The Twelve Days
of Autumn

The Twelve Days
of Autumn

by Jan Andrews
Illustrated by Susan Rennick Jolliffe

GSPH

For my Dad, Jim,
who loved birds and wished
he had been born with wings.

–Susan

To all who have loved our lake.

–*Jan*

On my first day of autumn,
the fall wind brought to me

A small home in a birch tree.

On my second day of autumn,
the fall wind brought to me

Two empty nests

And a small home in a birch tree.

On my third day of autumn,
the fall wind brought to me

Three woolly bears

Two empty nests

And a small home in a birch tree.

On my fourth day of autumn,
the fall wind brought to me

Four milkweed pods

Three woolly bears

Two empty nests

And a small home in a birch tree.

On my fifth day of autumn,
the fall wind brought to me

Five shrieking jays

Four milkweed pods

Three woolly bears

Two empty nests

And a small home in a birch tree.

On my sixth day of autumn,
the fall wind brought to me

Six groundhogs munching

Five shrieking jays

Four milkweed pods

Three woolly bears

Two empty nests

And a small home in a birch tree.

On my seventh day of autumn,
the fall wind brought to me

Seven frogs a-digging

Six groundhogs munching

Five shrieking jays

Four milkweed pods

Three woolly bears

Two empty nests

And a small home in a birch tree.

On my eighth day of autumn,
the fall wind brought to me

Eight ducks a-massing

Seven frogs a-digging

Six groundhogs munching

Five shrieking jays

Four milkweed pods

Three woolly bears

Two empty nests

And a small home in a birch tree.

On my ninth day of autumn,
the fall wind brought to me

Nine warblers flocking

Eight ducks a-massing

Seven frogs a-digging

Six groundhogs munching

Five shrieking jays

Four milkweed pods

Three woolly bears

Two empty nests

And a small home in a birch tree.

On my tenth day of autumn,
the fall wind brought to me

Ten snipe a-feeding

Nine warblers flocking

Eight ducks a-massing

Seven frogs a-digging

Six groundhogs munching

Five shrieking jays

Four milkweed pods

Three woolly bears

Two empty nests

And a small home in a birch tree.

On my eleventh day of autumn,
the fall wind brought to me

Eleven blackbirds thronging

Ten snipe a-feeding

Nine warblers flocking

Eight ducks a-massing

Seven frogs a-digging

Six groundhogs munching

Five shrieking jays

Four milkweed pods

Three woolly bears

Two empty nests

And a small home in a birch tree.

On my twelfth day of autumn,
the fall wind brought to me

Twelve geese a-calling

Eleven blackbirds thronging

Ten snipe a-feeding

Nine warblers flocking

Eight ducks a-massing

Seven frogs a-digging

Six groundhogs munching

Five shrieking jays

Four milkweed pods

Three woolly bears

Two empty nests

And a small home in a birch tree.

 # Facts – Common and Curious

Day 1 The home in the story is called a drey. It is made of leaves and twigs and maybe some pine needles. A drey gives warmth and shelter to its sleepy squirrel inhabitant during the worst of the winter cold.

Day 2 Autumn is the time for surprises. In trees and bushes, nests appear where they were once safely hidden by leaves. Nests are for babies and the babies have grown up and flown away long ago.

Day 3 Woolly bears are caterpillars that hibernate through the winter and spin their cocoons in spring. When a woolly bear is frightened, it curls around on itself so its head is hidden in the middle of its own circle. Woolly bears eventually become Isabella Tiger Moths.

Day 4 When the milkweed pods open, the seeds fly on the wind, ensuring new plants next season. Milkweeds are important – the only plants that the caterpillars of Monarch butterflies will eat.

Day 5 Blue jays have a pouch where their chins might be. Into that pouch, they stuff food – even peanuts in the shell! The food is then carried away to be hidden for times of scarcity.

Day 6 Groundhogs go into deep hibernation; their temperature falls to just above freezing, and their heart rate slows. The groundhog needs a good layer of body fat to survive this. That is what all the munching is about.

Day 7 Frogs dig into the earth or mud to hibernate. Their bodies may still freeze but they can thaw themselves out in the springtime – something humans would never be able to do.

Day 8 Ducks are like geese – they form into groups for migration and fly in Vees. Ducks find their way by responding to the sun, moon and stars, sounds and landmarks. Some even connect to the magnetism of the earth.

Day 9 Warblers come in over fifty different kinds. The yellow warbler is one of the ones you are most likely to see. It is a small bird but it travels a long way, flying as far as Central America when it migrates.

Day 10 If you are in open fields in spring or early summer and you hear a strange sound, look up. It may be a snipe, spreading its tail feathers and diving as it tries to attract a mate in a ritual known as winnowing.

Day 11 Why are some of the blackbirds in the picture brown? Because they are females and do not have the showy plumage of the males. Why do birds get together to fly south? Because there is safety in numbers.

Day 12 Geese follow the same migration routes every year. They travel at speeds of ninety kilometers an hour. The journey brings danger. Many of the geese that set out do not arrive. Those that do will be back in the spring, filling the skies with honking as they have for thousands of years.

Acknowledgements

Thanks go in abundance to the folks at General Store Publishing House who made working with the company such a pleasure. Mostly, we acknowledge our debt to the bugs, birds, beasts, flowers, trees, and other marvels around us. We both began our explorations by raising tadpoles in goldfish bowls when we were children. Neither of us can imagine life without so much to watch, to revel in, and learn from.

Jan Andrews
Susan Rennick Jolliffe

Jan Andrews and Susan Rennick Jolliffe at Taylor Lake

With their passion for the ways of nature, Jan Andrews and Susan Rennick Jolliffe make a perfect team. Jan not only supplies the story for *The Twelve Days of Autumn* but also the setting—the home she lives in at the end of a road on a lake in Eastern Ontario. Susan brings her exuberant love of detail and her concern with ensuring the flora and fauna she represents are authentic in every scene. The pair have been friends a long time. Collaborating on this follow-up to their earlier book, *The Twelve Days of Summer*, has brought them joy.

Both have their separate careers.

Jan is a well-known Canadian children's author and storyteller. She has written for all ages and won a number of awards. Further information: **www.janandrews.ca**. Hear her telling stories: **www.jansstorytellingclub.wordpress.com**.

Susan's work life includes creating humorous gallery sculptures, making art from recycled material with Eastern Ontario schoolchildren and illustrating children's books. She lives by the mighty Ottawa River with Bill and their dog Farley. To see more drawings and for more information: **www.susanrennickjolliffe.com**

GSPH

GENERAL STORE PUBLISHING HOUSE INC.

499 O'Brien Road, Renfrew, Ontario, K7V 3Z3
1.800.465.6072 • www.gsph.com

ISBN 978-1-77123-341-5

Copyright © Jan Andrews, Susan Rennick Jolliffe 2014

Printed by Image Digital Printing Ltd. dba The IDP Group
Printed and bound in Canada

Library and Archives Canada Cataloguing in Publication
Andrews, Jan, 1942-, author
 The twelve days of autumn / story by Jan Andrews ; illustrations
by Susan Rennick Jolliffe.
ISBN 978-1-77123-341-5 (pbk.)
 I. Jolliffe, Susan Rennick, illustrator II. Title.
PS8551.N37T827   2014   jC813'.54   C2014-906175-7

The Twelve Days
of Autumn

by Jan Andrews
Illustrated by Susan Rennick Jolliffe

TO ORDER MORE COPIES:

GENERAL STORE PUBLISHING HOUSE INC.
http://www.gsph.com • 1.800.465.6072 • Fax 1.613.432.3634